Arrrrgh! Slimosaur!

ALAN MACDONALD

Illustrations by Mark Beech

BLOOMSBURY

LONDON BERLIN NEW YORK SYDNEY

Contents

1 Boulderball..4

2 Who Dung It?...18

3 Tongue Tied..32

4 'If You Go Down to the Woods'.......49

5 Sticky!...62

6 A Bone to Pick...................................75

Arrrrgh! Slimosaur!

Bloomsbury Publishing, London, Berlin, New York and Sydney

First published in Great Britain in September 2010 by Bloomsbury Publishing Plc
36 Soho Square, London W1D 3QY

A CIP catalogue record of this book is available from the British Library

ISBN 978 1 4088 0335 6

FSC
Mixed Sources
Product group from well-managed
forests and other controlled sources
Cert no. SGS - COC - 2061
www.fsc.org
© 1996 Forest Stewardship Council

Typeset by Dorchester Typesetting Group Ltd
Printed in Great Britain by Clays Ltd, St Ives Plc

1 3 5 7 9 10 8 6 4 2

www.bloomsbury.com

7 We All Have to make Sacrifices......89

8 Saving Umily.................................102

9 Lair of the Slimosaur......................112

10 A Long Way Down........................123

11 Heads, You Lose..........................135

Long, long ago...

Really ages ago. The world was a wild and barren place. There were no houses or shops, no schools or teachers, no cars, flushing toilets or peanut-butter sandwiches. So many things didn't exist that to write them all down would fill every page of this book and leave no room for the story.

   If you want to imagine how the world was, imagine an endless landscape of mountains, forests, rocks and stones. In fact, stones lay everywhere, because this was . . .

1

THE STONE AGE

In the forests lived savage beasts — bears, snaggle-toothed tigers and woolly mammoths, which looked like elephants badly in need of a haircut. People generally avoided the forests. They lived together in tribes because it was safer that way and easier on the cooking. One such tribe was the Urks.

The Urks were a warlike race with bushy beards and hairy legs — especially some of the women. Their clothes were made of animal skins and they lived in caves high on a hill overlooking the Valley of Urk and the river winding through it. In one of these caves lived a boy called Iggy. He wasn't the tallest or the hairiest in his tribe, but what he did have was imagination, and this got him into a whole heap of trouble. That of course is another story ... Luckily it's the story that's about to begin ...

Chapter 1
Boulderball

Iggy crouched down and rubbed dirt into the palms of his hands.

He'd been looking forward to this day for weeks, imagining it, dreaming of it: the Junior Tribal Boulderball Tournament with his team, the Elks, as champions.

Now they were minutes away from the final, and only one thing stood in his way: the Rhinos. The Rhinos were Junior Champions and their captain was Snark, who happened to be Iggy's least favourite person in the world. Snark made no secret of the fact that he regarded Iggy as an annoying little pimple. Maybe it was because Iggy's uncle happened to be High Chief of the Urks, or maybe it was because he had what his dad called 'too many brains'; either way Snark hated him with a vengeance. That's why the game they were about to play wasn't just important, it was a chance to settle an old score.

Borg was waiting for the two captains at the boulder-off spot. It was typical, thought Iggy, that the referee for the final was Snark's dad. The ugpire was selected by the tribal elders, and Borg just happened to be Chief Elder.

Iggy glanced over at the crowd gathered at the edge of the pitch. It looked as if the whole tribe had turned out. Some of them had climbed trees to get a better view. It was a perfect day for boulderball, with heavy black clouds and a steady drizzle. Iggy could see his mum and dad in the crowd, standing behind Chief Hammerhead and his daughter, Umily. In front of Umily was the boulderball trophy, carved in the shape of a boulder. Iggy wondered if Umily was supporting the Elks today. He wondered too if this time he would win the toss. In boulderball, everything depended on it.

BOULDERBALL: A BEGINNER'S GUIDE
The Urks claim they invented the sport of boulderball,

though the Bludmug tribe play a similar game using the severed heads of their enemies. The rules, like most of the players, are pretty simple . . .

1. Two teams of six players attempt to roll the BOULDER into the opposing team's goal. The first team to score is the winner.

2. The boulder can be rolled by pushing, kicking or belting it with long wooden clubs called YOMPERS.

3. Goals are marked by two upright mammoth tusks called BONEPOSTS, spaced ten to twenty paces apart (depending on who is doing the pacing).

4. Players are permitted to BLOCK a moving boulder by putting their yomper or their body in its path. This can result in injury — or even death.

(Dead players must be removed from the pitch before

play may continue.)

5. *There are no FOULS in boulderball.*

6. *Team captains TOSS THE LIZARD to decide who has choice of ends. This can prove decisive (see point 8).*

7. *BOULDER OFF! A game starts with both teams standing behind their own boneposts. On the ugpire's signal, both teams run for the boulder and try to push it towards their opponent's goal.*

8. *PITCH — Boulderball is played on a hill, giving the team who has the slope a big advantage. Records from the 50,001—50,000 BC season show that teams playing uphill lost 99 per cent of all matches.*

*

Borg opened his hand to show them the small, blood-red lizard wriggling to escape.

'Call,' he said, tossing it high. Three pairs of eyes followed the red blob as it spun in the air.

'Heads!' shouted Snark.

The lizard hit the mud, landing on its back with its legs waggling helplessly. Snark nudged it with his foot, flipping the creature over on to its belly.

'Heads it is!' he cried triumphantly.

Iggy stared in disbelief. 'What? It was tails!'

Borg shook his head. 'Heads.'

'He cheated!' complained Iggy.

Borg picked up the lizard and pushed it under his nose.

'You questioning the ugpire's decision?' he growled.

Iggy swallowed. 'No, I just –'

'Good. Heads it is. Snark gets choice of ends.'

Snark tested the wind with his finger, pretending to think about it.

'We'll take the slope,' he said, grinning smugly.

Borg nodded. 'What boulder?'

Snark looked Iggy in the eyes. 'Hulka.'

There were three sizes of boulder used in tournaments – pebble, rubble and hulka. Hulka was the biggest and heaviest and as a rule only men

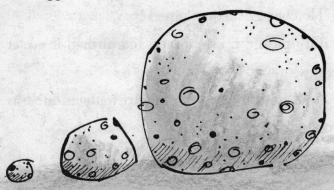

risked playing with it. Iggy watched three burly Urks roll the boulderball into position. It was big enough to flatten an entire village. He turned and walked back down the hill to where his team-mates were waiting anxiously.

'You won the toss?' asked Hubba.

Iggy shook his head. 'Not exactly. Snark cheated.'

Hubba groaned. 'We're dead.'

'No, we're not! Just remember what we talked about,' said Iggy. 'Speed and teamwork. Look at them – they think this is going to be a walkover.'

'It is,' muttered Hubba as they trudged back to take up their positions behind the boneposts. Iggy's heart was pounding. Teams playing uphill never won, certainly not against the Rhinos. But there was always a first time. He glanced over at Umily, who was whispering something to her father. A hush had fallen over the crowd. Borg stepped out on to the pitch holding a long curved horn and raised it to his lips. The two teams crouched, ready to run, yompers clutched in sweaty hands, the air thick with tension and drizzly rain.

BAWOOOOOOM!

The horn sounded. Iggy tore up the hill, knowing their only chance was to reach the boulder first.

'PUSH!' he yelled as he got there, using his yomper as a lever. Looking round, he realised he was talking to himself. Hubba and the others were a mile behind, still puffing up the hill. For the Rhinos, Snark had arrived, closely followed by the solid backing of Tug and Mauler. It was three against one. Snark levered the boulder with his yomper while the other two pushed, grunting and roaring with the effort. Iggy felt the boulder move – any second it was going to roll. Swiftly changing tactics, he dropped back to join the rest of his team.

'Make a wall!' he yelled.

Hubba looked at him. 'You're kidding.'

'Come on! We can block it!'

Iggy held his yomper upright in front of him to take the impact. Hubba and the others did the same, linking arms to form a human wall. The Rhinos gave a last grunt as they pushed the massive boulder down the slope. It rolled over and over, rumbling towards them like a giant black pudding.

'ARGHHH!' cried Hubba, panicking.

'DON'T MOVE!' yelled Iggy.

The wall broke at the last moment, scattering right and left. Iggy might have seen this if his eyes hadn't been closed. He was still heroically blocking the way when the boulderball flattened him. The crowd winced and looked away as Iggy's yomper splintered and he disappeared from sight. The boulderball sped on down the hill, rolling and bouncing over bumps, before finally crashing

into the goal, demolishing one of the boneposts.
The crowd rose to their feet as one.

'BOULDERRRR!'

Iggy didn't remember too much after that — only
the worried faces of his mum and dad looking
down on him and the sucking sound as they
pulled him out of the mud.

Later he joined the crowd that had gathered to
watch Snark collect the trophy.

'We was unlucky, that's all,' said Hubba, pat-
ting him on the shoulder. Iggy groaned. Just about
every part of him ached — his head, shoulders,
knees and elbows. It would be easier to say which
parts of him didn't ache.

Chief Hammerhead was congratulating Snark, who made a short speech, mainly in praise of himself. Finally Umily stepped forward to present him with the boulder-shaped trophy. Snark took it and leaned down to plant a kiss on her cheek. The crowd hooted and cheered while Umily pushed back her hair and flushed bright pink.

'UGH!' said Hubba. 'You see that?'

'Yes.' Iggy sighed.

'He kissed her!'

'I saw, OK?'

'Imagine that, bein' kissed by Snark! It'd be like kissing a warthog . . .'

Hubba found he was talking to himself. He stared in surprise after Iggy, who had stormed off up the hill, limping slightly.

The chants rang out across the valley as Snark lifted the knobbly trophy above his head.

'RHINOS! RHINOS! RHINOS!'

Chapter 2
Who Dung It?

The following day Iggy found his dad waiting for him impatiently outside the cave.

'Get your spear,' he grunted. 'We're going hunting.'

'Deadly!' said Iggy.

Dad had been promising to take him hunting for ages. Now he was a 'Son of Urk' he was old enough to accompany the men on their trips into the forest. Iggy hurried to fetch his spear and jaw-bone catapult.

*

An hour later they had crossed the river and were deep in the woods. Hubba had joined them, along with Chief Hammerhead, who insisted on giving his nephew the benefit of his experience. It was rare these days for the grizzled old Chief to set foot in the forest, but Iggy knew that no one was better at tracking and hunting. It was often said that the Chief had killed seven bears before he was old enough to grow a beard. (It was Hammerhead who often said it.)

It was nearing dusk as the four of them threaded their way through the forest. The trees cast long shadows that to Iggy looked like many-headed monsters. He tried to listen to what his dad was telling him about tracking animals.

'Remember, a tracker don't talk, he uses his eyes and ears.'

'And nose,' added Hammerhead, tapping his own large nose. 'See that, boys? A hunter's nose, that is. Runs in the family.' He sniffed loudly.

'And another thing,' said Dad, 'when you're hunting, never make a noise.'

'No – or you'll frighten off all the beasties,' agreed Hammerhead as he crashed through the undergrowth like a rhinoceros. He stopped and wiped his brow. 'Whew! I'm frazzled! Shall

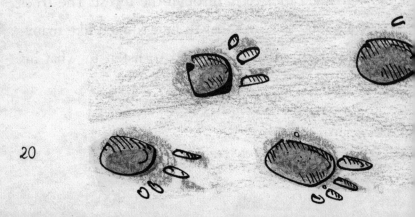

us go back now?'

'Back?' said Dad. 'We only just come out!'

They rested awhile, the Chief propping himself against a tree. Dad wandered off by himself. Iggy saw him squat down in the mud and examine the ground. He beckoned them over.

'See them?' he said, pointing. 'Tracks.'

Iggy crouched beside him eagerly. There were enormous footprints in the mud.

'What are they?' he asked.

'Bear tracks,' said Hammerhead, coming over to join them.

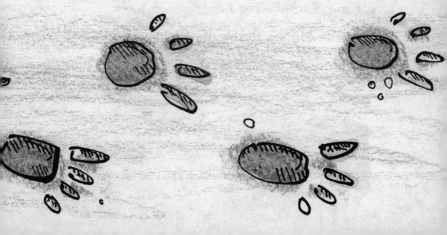

Dad ignored him. 'You got to learn how to read 'em. Look close. What d'you see?'

'Footprints,' said Iggy. 'Big ones.'

'What else?'

Iggy traced the outline of the footprint with his hand. It was huge. Bigger than a human head – even his uncle's head.

'It's sort of round,' he said. 'And there are four little marks.'

'Bear claws.' Hammerhead nodded. 'I were about your age when I killed my first bear. Woke up and found this whopping great grizzler about to eat me. Know what I did?'

Iggy and Hubba shook their heads.

'Tickled him. Bears can't abide tickling.

Especially not their feet.'

Dad rolled his eyes. 'For Urk's sake! I'm trying to learn 'em something!'

'I *AM* learning 'em,' said Hammerhead.

'It's not a bear, Hammy, it's too big! How many footprints you see?'

Hammerhead got down on his knees to count. 'Two,' he said eventually.

'Two,' said Dad. 'Which means he's walking on *TWO* legs.'

Hammerhead tapped his nose wisely. 'Ah. Bears is clever like that.'

They followed the tracks through the forest. It wasn't difficult since whatever-it-was had trampled down the plants and bushes in its path. At last they came to a clearing where flies buzzed and there was a strong, pungent smell. Iggy and Hubba hung back while Dad crouched over a gigantic brown splodge, prodding it with a stick.

'Droppings,' he muttered. 'You can tell a lot from droppings. Take a look, boys.'

Iggy reluctantly went closer. No one had warned him that learning to hunt involved poking around in piles of poo. He hoped he wouldn't be asked to pick it up. Dad explained that you could identify an animal from the size, shape and texture of its droppings.

Dad looked at Hammerhead and raised his eyebrows. 'You still say it's a bear?'

'Could be,' said the Chief. 'Or a mammoth.'

'Mammoths eat leaves. Whatever this ate, it weren't no leaf. There's scabby bits of bone in it.'

1 Rabbits/Hares

2 Bears, hyenas, racoons

3 Deer

4 Snaggle-toothed tiger

5 Woolly mammoth

Iggy glanced at Hubba, whose eyes were darting around like tadpoles. The light was fading fast and the air had grown cooler.

Hammerhead pulled at his thick red beard. 'Maybe we should head back,' he said. 'I mean, if the boys are scared like.'

'I'm not scared,' said Hubba quickly.

'Nor me,' said Iggy. This wasn't strictly true, but he didn't want to return empty-handed from his first hunting trip.

Dad nodded. 'Let me go first then. Quiet mind, and keep your eyes skinned.'

'Not a sound,' agreed Hammerhead. 'Quiet as bats. Or snakes, which is quieter.'

They crept forward in single file, pushing their

way through giant ferns which towered over their heads. A fly crawled up Iggy's neck and he brushed it away with his hand. Behind him he could hear Hubba breathing heavily. Iggy reminded himself that nothing bad could happen, not while they were with Dad and the Chief. Besides, he wanted to find out what kind of creature had made the tracks. If it wasn't a bear or a mammoth, it had to be something pretty huge. Dad halted suddenly and raised a hand.

'Are we stopping?' boomed Hammerhead.

'Shhh!' Dad crouched down and signalled for them to follow his example. He was peering through the branches at something ahead. Iggy crept forward to join him, his heart racing. A low

drone hummed in his ears. In a patch of sunlight
flies were swarming in a dark cloud, buzzing over
something that lay on the ground. Dad stole out
from the bushes and Iggy followed him, gripping
his spear tightly. Whatever it was, there wasn't
much of it left – just a pile of bones and flesh with
no sign of the head. Strangest of all, the carcass
was covered in a sticky green slime – as if a giant

had sneezed over it.

Iggy heard a noise and turned in time to see his uncle throwing up in the bushes.

'Sorry,' said the Chief, wiping his mouth. 'Swallowed a fly.'

Dad crouched down to examine the sticky pile of bones.

'What do you think it was, Dad?' asked Iggy.

'Hard to say.' Dad stood up and frowned. 'Maybe we should get back.'

'But what about the tracks?' persisted Iggy.

'Leave 'em. Too dark now anyhow,' said Dad.

They hurried back through the forest, Iggy and Hubba having to run to keep up. Nobody spoke much, not even Hammerhead, who was too out of breath. Iggy's head was bursting with questions, but he had the feeling they would have to wait for another day. Whatever had eaten the something-or-other back there, it wasn't a bear or a mammoth.

Chapter 3
Tongue Tied

A week passed, but there were no more hunting trips. In fact, Iggy's dad had forbidden him to go to the forest or even to cross the river. When Iggy asked why his dad just said, 'Because I say' and quickly changed the subject. With no hunting, there was rarely any meat at suppertime. Mum said they'd just have to make do with what there was — which was mostly a stew of bitter roots and the odd gristly bone.

Iggy soon grew tired of hanging around the

cave, especially since his grumma had started coming round a lot lately, usually at mealtimes. Iggy's grumma was a sour old woman with a bush of grey hair and a face like a wrinkled prune. She had a way of looking at Iggy as if she knew he was up to something.

He decided to go down to the river. If they couldn't hunt, there was always fish, though catching them was a problem.

'Where are you off to?' demanded his mum.

'Nowhere,' said Iggy. 'Just the river.'

Mum grunted. 'Unh. Well, mind you don't go no further.'

A thin complaining voice wailed from inside the cave.

'Wait a minute, Grumma!' sighed Mum.

'Anyway, I'll be with Hubba,' said Iggy, turning to go.

'I don't care who you're with — keep out that forest!' Mum yelled after him.

Iggy walked down the hill, trying not to think about how empty his stomach felt (breakfast that morning had been lizard tails). As he approached the river, he saw someone on the bank. It wasn't Hubba as he'd expected; it was Umily. Iggy hadn't seen her since the day of the boulderball tournament, when he hadn't exactly covered himself in glory. She was kneeling on the muddy bank with her back to him, staring intently at something in the water. He wondered if he should go back or risk trying to speak to her. While he was trying to decide, he spotted a patch of dandelions growing under a tree. Maybe he should pick some for Umily as a present? At least he'd have a reason to speak to her. He gathered a large bunch. They were rather droopy, but that couldn't be helped.

'Hello!' he said, trying to sound as if he'd only just noticed her. Umily didn't even turn round. She kept staring at the river. Iggy saw now that she had one arm in the water.

Iggy tapped her lightly on the shoulder. 'Umily?'

She gave a yelp and sort of jumped – which is difficult when you're kneeling down and dangerous if you're on a riverbank. Before Iggy could grab her she overbalanced and toppled in head first. She came up spluttering and coughing. Iggy thought she looked a bit cross, not to mention pretty wet.

'You . . . you clumsy bonehead!' she spluttered.

Iggy stared. Him clumsy? She was the one who had just fallen in a river!

'What're you doing, creeping up on me? I'm soaked!'

'You look . . . nice,' said Iggy. 'Just a bit, well, drippy.'

'*Drippy?*'

He seemed to be making things worse. Umily waded to the bank and Iggy reached out a hand to help her. She ignored him and scrambled out by herself.

'What are they?' She was pointing at the dandelions, which he'd completely forgotten.

'Oh, they're, um . . . flowers.' His voice had gone croaky. He sounded like a frog. He held out the bunch of droopy dandelions.

Umily stared as if he was offering her a plate of slugs.

'They're dead,' she said.

'Are they?' Iggy hadn't even realised flowers *could* be dead. In any case, what had given him the idea that Umily might want some? She was a chief's daughter; she could skin a rabbit without fainting.

'Look,' he said.
'They're magic.
Watch this.'

He took a deep
breath and blew.
Dandelion seeds
filled the air like tiny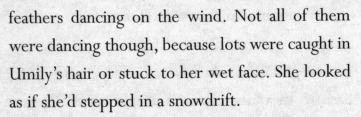
feathers dancing on the wind. Not all of them
were dancing though, because lots were caught in
Umily's hair or stuck to her wet face. She looked
as if she'd stepped in a snowdrift.

'Sorry!' He tried to brush the bits out of her
hair, but she pushed him off. The feathery seeds
were still floating around in a blizzard. Iggy
caught one in his hand and examined it.

'If you had thousands of these, you could fly,' he said.

'What?'

'I was just thinking. You could jump off a cliff and fly. Like a bird.'

'That I'd like to see,' she said.

'Me flying?'

'You jumping off a cliff.'

Umily was shivering and brushing at her hair to get rid of all the seeds. Iggy noticed her looking past his shoulder, up the hill. He turned to see Snark coming their way, carrying a spear.

Snark leapt the last few yards, landing beside them. 'You're wet,' he said, staring at Umily.

'Yes. Somebody pushed me in.'

Snark turned on Iggy. 'What you gawping at, face-ache?'

'Nothing,' said Iggy.

Snark glared, perhaps considering whether to throw him in the river. He evidently decided it wasn't worth the effort.

'Ready?' he said to Umily. 'It's further up. Best spot on the river.'

'Best for what?' asked Iggy.

'Catching fish. What d'you think?' said Umily.

Iggy flushed. So that was why Umily had been staring at the water so intently! She had been fishing. Catching fish by hand required patience, skill and total silence, which he'd shattered by scaring off every fish within a mile. No wonder

Umily had looked cross!

'See you around then, boulder boy,' said Snark, as he and Umily set off upstream. Iggy watched them go. He sighed heavily and began to trudge back up the hill. If Umily wanted to go fishing with a blathermouth like Snark, that was her business. *What do I care?* he thought, kicking a stone aside. He tossed away the droopy dandelion stalks. Despite his gloom, his thoughts turned back to flying. Wouldn't it be amazing to soar like a bird, gliding and swooping through the sky? He imagined jumping off a high cliff clutching a bunch of a thousand dandelions while a crowd watched from below.

It would never work.

*

Back at the cave, there didn't seem to be anyone around. His mum had left a deerskin hanging out to dry. It was stretched on a frame between two poles, flapping like a bird in the wind. Iggy stared at it thoughtfully for a while. Maybe dandelions weren't the only way . . .

A minute later he stood on a rock holding the deerskin by two corners. He waited for a strong gust of wind and let the skin go, tossing it as high as he could.

FLUMP! The skin ballooned out like a ship's sail, then floated gently back to earth.

'Your ma's gonna be pleased,' said a voice behind him. Iggy turned to find Grumma watching him from the mouth of the cave. She made a habit of creeping up on people like this.

'Oh, Grumma, I was just . . .'

'Throwing skins around.' Grumma nodded.

'. . . Just borrowing it.' He picked up the deer-skin and hung it back over the frame. There was a dirty brown stain in the middle. He rubbed at it with his hand, which only managed to make it bigger.

Grumma squatted by the fire, watching him all the while like a beady-eyed toad. She had dark hairs on her top lip. If she got much older, Iggy thought she could probably grow a full beard.

'Been to the forest?' she asked.

'No, Grumma. You know I'm not allowed.'

Grumma grunted. 'I know what I hear.'

'What do you mean?' asked Iggy.

'Never you mind.' She gave him a sly, calculating look. 'I hear 'em talking when they think I'm asleep.'

'Who?'

'Who d'you think?'

'Mum and Dad? What were they talking about?'

Grumma smiled, crinkling her eyes into dark slits. 'Never you mind. Caves have ears.'

'Please, Grumma! I won't tell anyone.'

She beckoned him over to sit beside the fire. For a while she was silent, picking at her pointed yellow teeth.

'That day in the forest – you seen it, didn't you?' she said.

'We saw tracks,' replied Iggy. 'And poo. And the bones of something. But I don't know what killed it.'

Grumma nodded. 'Sticky bones, was they? Slimy, like the innards of an egg?'

'How did you know?'

She gave him a look. 'Ah. Just as I thought. It's come back.'

'What has?'

'The creature. The beast.'

'You know about it? Is it a mammoth?'

'No, boy. A hundred times worse 'n that.'

'Then what?'

Grumma looked around to check that no one was within earshot. She dropped her voice.

'Ever hear of a slimosaur?'

Iggy shook his head. He had heard of snaggle-toothed tigers and woolly rhinos with savage horns, but his parents had never said anything about a slimosaur.

'What's it like?' he asked.

Grumma laughed, showing her pink gums. 'You think I'd be here talking to you if I ever seen it? I know this – it come before. Long ago, when I were a girl.'

'It came here?' said Iggy, astonished. 'To the valley?'

'To the forest. Eight . . . nine of our tribe was took – most of 'em young'uns. Not one were seen again. Not one.'

Iggy shivered, hugging his knees. 'You think they were eaten?'

'All we found was their bones. Bones and nasty slime.' She sat back and warmed her blue-veined hands at the fire.

'Still, not to worry,' she added cheerfully. 'Keep out of the forest, and maybe you'll live. Now where's that mother of yours? I'm hungry as a crow.'

Iggy looked away, staring across the valley at

the mist rising off the Forest of Urk. Somewhere out there he imagined an ugly great beast, fast asleep and dreaming of tasty Urk children.

Chapter 4
'If You Go Down to the Woods'

Breakfast next morning was leftover bone stew — though not much was left over. Afterwards Iggy and Hubba set out in search of something more filling to eat. Finding nothing, they stopped under some trees for a rest. Iggy turned over a large stone, uncovering a sea of wriggling earthworms.

Hubba scooped up a handful and held them in the palm of his hand. 'Have some,' he said.

Iggy shook his head. 'No, thanks. You go ahead.'

'Tasty, worms is. You got to swallow 'em in one, mind.'

Hubba crammed the worms into his mouth. A pink tail dangled from one corner of his lips and he sucked it up like a piece of spaghetti.

Iggy's stomach heaved. He was just as starving as Hubba, but he had never been able to face eating worms. Grubs and maggots were the same. His mum said he was a mealy-mouthed fusspot. What he would give now for a leg of roast boar! It had been almost two weeks since he'd tasted meat of any kind, and he was sure his ribs were beginning to stick out. Even the best hunters in the tribe, like his dad, were too scared to venture into the forest. Families were living on grubs, roots and bones. Occasionally someone caught a lizard, which they cooked on a stick for supper, dividing it between four or five people.

'Yumberries!' said Hubba, licking his lips. 'I know where there's heaps of yumberries.'

Iggy stared at him. 'Why didn't you say so before?'

'Know that bank along by the stream? Yumberries grows there like weeds. More 'n you can eat.'

'Which stream?' asked Iggy. 'Not the one in the forest?'

Hubba nodded.

Iggy let out a long sigh like a balloon going down. For a moment his hopes had been raised. He'd imagined cramming fistfuls of ripe yumberries into his mouth, the purple juice running down his chin. He lay back on the grass and groaned.

'Hubba, we're not allowed in the forest. You know that!'

'But yumberries, Iggy, think of it.'

'My mum would never let us. Yours neither. They'd go mad if we even asked.'

Hubba propped himself up on one elbow. 'Then maybe we don't. We slip out when they're asleep.'

'At night?' said Iggy. 'You want to go to the forest at night?'

'Why not?'

'What if we bump into the . . . thing? You heard what my grumma said – it eats children!'

Hubba snorted. 'Your grumma's barmy. She told me her hair's falling out.'

'It is.'

'Oh. Anyway, it's all hogslop. Has anyone ever seen the beast?'

'We saw those tracks,' said Iggy.

Hubba shrugged. 'Could've been anything. It's not like we'd be going far. Only to the stream.'

Iggy still looked doubtful. He didn't like the idea of going to the forest. Certainly not at night when it would be dark and creepy, not to mention dangerous. All the same, he didn't want Hubba thinking he was scared – and he was hungry. Unbearably hungry.

'Yumberries . . .' Hubba sighed. 'Fat, juicy yumberries, big as your thumb.'

'Stop it!'

'Hanging in plumptious bunches . . .'

'All right!' groaned Iggy. 'We'll go. But only as far as the stream. We pick what we can carry and come straight back, all right?'

Hubba grinned. He wondered how many berries he could actually carry. Maybe he'd take a sack.

*

Late that night, Iggy pushed back the furs that he slept under. He'd been listening for some time to make sure his parents were asleep. He could hear his mum's heavy snoring and knew she would be splayed on her back like a starfish. It would take an invasion of clog-dancing mammoths to wake her. He crept from the cave, stepping carefully over his dad's legs.

Outside, the moon had painted the hillside a ghostly grey. Iggy peered into the darkness, hoping Hubba might have forgotten the plan and he wouldn't have to go through with it.

'Iggy? That you?' hissed a voice.

Ten minutes later they were wading across the

ice-cold river. Iggy had brought a flaming torch dipped in animal fat, something his dad had taught him. It should burn for hours.

Hubba led the way as they hurried through the trees. At night the forest was an altogether different place, full of strange shapes and unfamiliar sounds. An owl hooted in the darkness and something scurried into the undergrowth, perhaps a badger or maybe a wolf going to fetch his friends.

'You said it wasn't far,' whispered Iggy.

'It's not. Just a bit further,' said Hubba.

'We ought to go back.'

'Yumberries . . .' said Hubba. 'Keep thinking of yumberries.'

*

At last, just as Iggy was beginning to think they were lost, they stumbled upon the stream. A tangle of thorny bushes grew nearby and, as Hubba had predicted, berries hung in huge clusters, laced with dewy cobwebs. Before long Iggy had forgotten that he had wanted to go back. He was busy plucking the largest berries and filling his empty stomach. They held a contest to see which of them could cram most yumberries into his mouth at once. Hubba held the record with seventeen. Iggy was about to try to go one better when he heard a sound like a tree falling.

THUD!

His heart stopped beating. 'What was that?' he whispered.

Hubba wiped his purple mouth. 'A squirrel?'

THUD! THUD! The ground shook and a shower of leaves fell.

'Um . . . two squirrels?'

A wave of panic swept over Iggy. He suddenly saw the utter foolishness of entering a deep dark forest when you know flesh-eating monsters are on the prowl. It was the kind of thing only Hubba could have suggested, but Iggy's judgement had been clouded by hunger and the promise of yumberries.

They stood very still and listened, not knowing which direction it was coming from.

CRASHHHH!

They both dived to the ground. Iggy almost

dropped the torch.

'Keep still,' he hissed. 'Maybe it won't see us.'

'GROOARGHHHHHHHH!'

The roar echoed through the forest, sending rabbits diving into their holes and bears hiding under their beds. Hubba's nerve snapped and he broke from the bushes.

'Hubba! No!' cried Iggy.

Suddenly a shadow loomed out of the sky. Looking up, he saw the thing lumber past on two powerful legs. Green scales glinted in the moonlight, and through the treetops he glimpsed an enormous head and one yellow eye. A moment

later it was gone from sight, crashing off through the forest like an armour-plated tank.

'IGGY!' wailed Hubba, his voice rising in terror.

Iggy ran towards the sound, his heart pounding, fearing that he was already too late.

Chapter 5
Sticky!

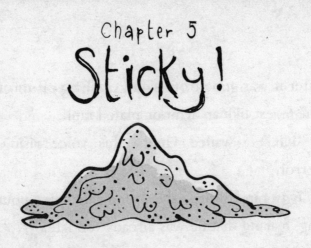

Iggy burst through the trees into a clearing and came upon the sight he'd dreaded. The slimosaur was crouched over a glistening heap on the ground. The heap wasn't moving, but from the dirty feet Iggy could tell it was Hubba.

The sheer size of the creature took his breath away. It was like a green lizard that had swallowed a magic growing potion. It stood on two powerful legs as thick as tree trunks, with a long neck, gleaming yellow eyes and a head crowned with ugly lumps like stumpy horns. Iggy had only seconds to take any of this in as the creature turned its great head towards him and let out a savage roar.

He knew he had two choices – to stay and fight, or run for his life. The beast had shifted round to face him. Gobbets of sticky drool dripped from its mouth. Suddenly it lumbered forward. Iggy thrust the torch flame in its face, yelling something like:

'WOOOARGHHH!'

To his amazement the slimosaur reared back, bellowing like a bull. The next moment it turned tail and charged through the trees, vanishing as suddenly as it had appeared.

Iggy stood still for a moment, breathing heavily and trembling all over. Then he remembered Hubba and went back to the sticky heap under the trees, hardly daring to look. It stirred and let out a groan.

'Hubba? You all right?' asked Iggy.

Hubba stuck out a hand and pushed himself upright. He was covered from head to toe in a revolting slime that stank of bad eggs. It was a pale green snot colour and stuck to his hair like chewing gum. Gunk dripped from his nose and gummed up his eyes as he blinked like a newborn chick.

'Gloop,' he mumbled. 'Glub . . . gonna . . .'

'What?'

'Gonna be . . .'

Iggy leapt back just in time as Hubba vomited a purple torrent of yumberries.

He wiped his mouth. '. . . sick,' he panted.

On the way back they stopped at the river, where Hubba washed off as much of the foul-smelling slime as he could. Iggy watched him from the bank.

'I still don't understand,' he said. 'Why didn't it eat you?'

'Maybe I don't taste so good.'

'Or maybe I frightened it off with the torch,' suggested Iggy. 'Maybe it's scared of fire.'

Hubba grunted. 'Didn't look scared to me.' He waded to the bank and scrambled out. 'Anyway. Thanks.'

'For what?'

'For saving me.'

Iggy shrugged. 'Forget it. You would've done the same for me.'

'Yeah,' said Hubba. 'Probably.'

Iggy glanced up at the sky. Dawn was on the way. If they hurried, they could still make it back to the caves before anyone noticed they were missing.

*

The following night Chief Hammerhead called a meeting at the Standing Stone. All the tribe was there and Iggy sensed a mood of simmering discontent. It was weeks since anyone had set foot in the forest, and meat had become as rare as lavender-scented soap. The rows of faces listened in grim silence as Hammerhead outlined the seriousness of the situation. Everyone had heard the terrifying rumours about the beast in the forest.

Once the hubbub had died down the Chief stood up and asked the elders for their advice. There was a good deal of head nodding, beard tugging and puzzled looks from one or two who hadn't heard the question. Some of the elders

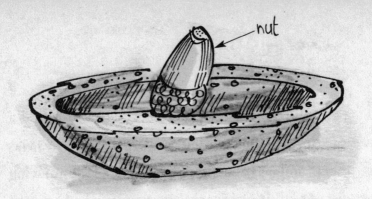

nut

were so old they had difficulty remembering their
own names, let alone what they were meant to be
discussing.

'If you ask me, it's nuts,' began one elder.

'I don't see why,' said Hammerhead.

'No, nuts! We should all eat nuts.'

'Berries are juicier,' said a second elder. 'I has-
n't tasted berries for weeks.'

'But nuts are better for you,' maintained the
first. 'Look at squirrels.'

'Where?'

'No, they eat nuts.'

'Or grubs. What about grubs?' put in a third.

This might have led to a long discussion of what the elders liked for breakfast, but it was interrupted by an axe blade thudding into the ground. It belonged to Borg, Chief of the Elders.

'For the love of Urk!' he thundered. 'We hasn't come here to talk about nuts and berries! There's families starving, living on scraggy old bones.'

There were low murmurs of agreement.

'For weeks now we been cooped up like animals,' said Borg. 'We can't hunt. We can't even go to the forest. If this goes on, we'll all be dead before winter's out!' Borg paused for effect and stepped forward into the firelight before continuing. 'So let me ask a question. What's our Chief going to do about it?'

This was greeted with an angry roar, especially from some of the women. All eyes turned to Hammerhead, who looked a little startled. The truth was, he often drifted off during tribal meetings and he'd been thinking about whether he should cut his beard or let it grow to his waist. He had no idea what to do about the slimosaur, which was why he hoped the elders would come up with a solution. The best thing, of course, would be to kill it, but he wasn't about to try that himself. A heavy silence hung over the gathering as Hammerhead rose slowly to his feet.

'As you all know,' he said, 'I am your Chief. High Chief of the Urks. So I been giving this a good deal of thought.' He stared into the fire for a while.

'And?' said Borg impatiently.

'Never think too much,' said Hammerhead wisely. 'If you think too much, then you think thinks that you thought you thought but you . . . um only thought them.'

People were looking confused. Hammerhead was a bit confused himself. Luckily Gaga the Wise stood up at this point and came to his rescue.

'I think I see what the Chief is trying to say.'

'Do you?' asked Hammerhead, astonished.

'Yes. What we should be asking is, why has the beast returned?'

'Returned?' said Borg. 'You mean this weren't the first time?'

Gaga shook his silvery head. 'It happened before, many moons ago. A few of you here may remember.'

Most of the Urks looked blank, but some older heads, including that of Iggy's grumma, were nodding gravely.

'What did you do then?' demanded Borg.

'Do? We did nothing,' replied Gaga the Wise. 'And many Urks were taken. That is why this time we mustn't make the same mistake. We must be bold and take action.'

'Just what I were about to say,' agreed Hammerhead.

'What action?' asked Borg.

'The beast is hungry. It thirsts for blood,' said Gaga the Wise. 'Very well, then give it blood. Choose one of our tribe to offer as a sacrifice.'

'S-sacrifice?' stammered Hammerhead.

'Yes, to the Spirits of the Ancestors. They will protect us and drive the beast away.'

Hammerhead had gone rather pale.

'So what you're saying is . . . take someone to the forest and leave 'em? To be eaten?'

Gaga the Wise nodded. 'I fear it's our only hope.'

Hammerhead cleared his throat and looked at

the rows of startled faces. Everyone had fallen deathly silent.

'Well,' he said, rubbing his hands, 'any volunteers?'

Chapter 6
A Bone to Pick

'But I don't want to be eaten!' wailed Snark.

'Shut up, boy. No one's gonna eat you,' snapped Borg.

'How do you know? What if I'm chosen?'

They were sitting near the mouth of their cave. Borg was examining a collection of fish bones by the light of a low fire. He was the one who had suggested that the sacrificial victim should be chosen by the ancient Urk practice of 'picking bones' – whoever drew the shortest bone (known as the Dark Bone) would die a horrible death.

All male Urks were to take part in the ceremony, which explained why Snark was in a state of panic. He didn't want to die young and he certainly didn't want to be sacrificed to a flesh-eating monster. His dad however didn't seem the slightest bit concerned. Borg was busy working at one of the fish bones, using a small flint cutter.

'What are you doing?' asked Snark.

'Making sure there's no mistake.'

Snark looked puzzled. 'I thought it were luck,' he said. 'Whoever draws the Dark Bone gets chosen.'

'Luck has nothing to do with it,' snapped Borg. He held the fish bone up to the light, revealing a small groove running across its centre.

'See that? The Dark Bone. That's so I can tell her apart.'

'Why?' asked Snark.

'So the right person gets it. Understand?'

Snark wasn't sure he did. 'But, Dad, anyone could choose that bone. I could!'

'You won't,' said Borg, 'because someone holds the bones while you pick. And that someone'll be me.' He held the fish bone closer to the fire, letting it catch the light. 'This little beauty is for our Chief.'

Snark frowned. 'What if he don't pick that one?'

'Oh, he will,' said Borg. 'I'll make sure.'

'Then . . . he'll be the sacrifice? The Chief is going to die?'

Borg smiled a wolfish smile.

Of course, thought Snark. It all made sense. For years his father had been scheming to become High Chief, and with Hammerhead out of the way there would be no one to stop him. He had to admit it was a brilliant plan. No one would suspect foul play, because they would all witness their Chief draw the Dark Bone himself. Hammerhead would die because the Spirits of the Ancestors had chosen him. It was tragic but it couldn't be helped.

That night the tribe gathered at the Standing Stone in sombre mood. The fire crackled and spat, casting an eerie red glow over the circle around it. People spoke in low voices. They were all brooding on the same unspoken fear, wondering if they would be chosen. Seated next to his dad, Iggy caught sight of Umily across the circle. He was surprised to see her beside the Chief, since girls normally didn't take part in tribal ceremonies. Knowing Umily, she had probably insisted on taking her chances along with the men. He saw her smile shyly and turned his head to see Snark grinning at her like an ape. Iggy resisted a strong urge to throw a rock at him.

The murmur of voices died away as Borg stepped into the middle of the circle. In his hand was a large sheaf of bones. He explained in a

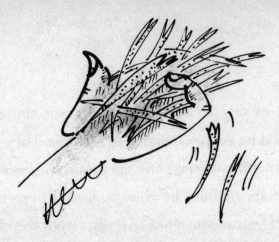

solemn voice how the ceremony would work. He would pass around the circle until every person had drawn a bone, beginning with those nearest the Standing Stone and ending with the Chief and the elders. There were a few rumbles of discontent and someone raised a hand.

'What do we do with the bone once we got one?'

'Just keep it till the end,' replied Borg.

'Can we suck it?'

'No!'

'What if we draw the Dark Bone?' asked someone else. 'Do we call out or put up a hand?'

'Just keep the dung thing,' sighed Borg wearily. 'We'll know who's got it at the end. Any more stupid questions? Good, then let's begin.'

He held the fish bones bunched in his fist so only the tops were visible. No one (apart from him) would be able to tell which was the Dark Bone. Slowly Borg began to walk round the circle, stopping for each person to draw a bone from his hand. The silence stretched out longer than a rubber band. Iggy watched the faces, seeing fear in their eyes and then relief when they saw that they were safe. On and on went the ceremony as the number of bones in Borg's hand grew smaller and smaller. Snark took his turn and triumphantly held up a long bone for everyone to see.

Soon there were fewer than a dozen bones left. So far no one had drawn the Dark Bone, unless they were keeping very quiet about it. Iggy watched his dad draw, knowing it was his turn next. He closed his eyes and asked the Spirits of the Ancestors to guide him. Ideally he would have liked letters of fire spelling out: 'Pick the one on the left', but right now he'd settle for a bit of luck.

Borg bent towards him, the fish bones in his fist sticking up like the quills of some tiny animal. Iggy's heart thumped as he reached out to pick.

Eeny meeny miny . . .

'Get on with it!' snapped Borg.

Iggy chose. He let out a long breath as he saw the bone was long and thin. Borg moved on to Umily and the elders before coming to Hammerhead. No one noticed his hands come together for a moment like a magician's. The Chief hesitated. One bone, bearing an almost invisible mark, was poking up from the rest of the bunch in Borg's fist, making it look longer than the rest. Hammerhead grasped it.

Iggy heard the gasp from those close enough to see. The Chief was staring in horror at the bone in his hand, which was jagged and shorter than a toothpick.

'The Dark Bone,' breathed Borg. 'Oh, what a pity!'

The blood had drained from Hammerhead's face. 'No! Wait . . .' he mumbled. 'For the love of Urk!'

'There's some mistake,' said Iggy's dad, rising to his feet.

Borg shook his head. 'No mistake. The Spirits have chosen. See for yourself.'

He took the bone from Hammerhead's trembling hand and held it up so the whole tribe could see.

'Ahhhhhh!' cried the Urks, craning their necks to get a better look.

'Wait!' called a loud voice. Heads turned to see

who had spoken. Umily had left her place in the circle.

'That's not the Dark Bone,' she said. 'This is.'

'Nonsense!' snapped Borg. He took the bone from Umily and compared it with the one drawn by the Chief. There was no question that Umily's bone was shorter.

'But . . . But that's not possible,' stammered Borg.

'Why not?' demanded Umily angrily. 'Why shouldn't the Spirits choose me – a Chief's daughter? Who says I'm not worthy?'

No one answered. When it came to choosing a sacrifice, the Urks felt Umily was just as worthy as any of them. The only person who disagreed was Hammmerhead, who felt it was a terrible waste of a good daughter.

'No!' he sobbed. 'Not Umily! Take one of the elders — they'll be dead soon anyway!'

It was no use. Much as he begged and pleaded, there was nothing he could do. Umily had drawn the Dark Bone and tomorrow night she would be sacrificed to save the tribe.

'I still can't believe it,' said Iggy as they climbed the hill to their caves.

'No,' agreed Hubba. 'Don't seem right.'

'I mean, why Umily? She's . . . she's . . .'

'A girl,' said Hubba.

'Yes! You can't sacrifice her to a blood-sucking

monster. It's not right!'

Hubba shook his head. 'I know. Specially as she cheated.'

Iggy stopped in his tracks. 'What?'

'She cheated. I were sitting right near her. She snapped her bone in half.'

'You're kidding? Why didn't you say something before?'

Hubba shrugged his shoulders. 'Not much I could say. Everyone were yammering at once. Anyway, she knows what she's doing.'

Iggy stared. 'No, she doesn't! Don't you see? She did it to save her father! Oh, Umily!'

'Yes.' Hubba sighed. 'Umily, dumily . . . died for her fumily.'

'HUBBA!' shouted Iggy.

'What?'

'Haven't you been listening? They're going to sacrifice her! She'll be eaten alive!'

'Well, yes. But not if someone were to save her, like.'

'Who's going to do that?'

'You.'

'ME?' cried Iggy.

'Yes. You like her, don't you?'

Iggy went bright pink. His mouth opened and closed.

'It's simple,' Hubba went on. 'All you've got to do is kill the slimosaur. I reckon she'll be pretty grateful.'

Chapter 7
We All Have to make Sacrifices

The next morning was the day of the sacrifice and Iggy got up early to go in search of Umily. He eventually found her sitting all alone by the river. She looked paler than usual, as if she hadn't slept much the previous night.

'Oh,' she said, looking up, 'it's you.'

Iggy sat down beside her on the bank and for a while they watched the river go by in silence.

'How's the flying coming on?' she asked.

'I'm still working on it,' said Iggy. 'I've given up on dandelions.'

'Pity.'

The river went by some more.

'You don't have to go,' said Iggy at last.

Umily sighed and tore up a handful of grass. 'Someone has to. And I were chosen.'

'That's what I mean. You weren't, were you?'

Umily looked at him sharply. 'What do you mean?'

'I know what you did. You cheated.'

'Why on Urk would I do that?'

'Hubba saw you. He told me.'

Umily stared at the ground and tore up another handful of grass. At this rate there wouldn't be any grass left.

'So what you going to do? Tell on me?' she said.

'Of course not,' said Iggy. 'But if you go through with this, you'll get yourself killed.'

Umily winced. 'What else could I do?' she said. 'They were going to send my dad.'

'But he's the Chief!' said Iggy. 'He's a great warrior, a legend. Surely he can look after himself?'

'Dad?' Umily laughed bitterly. 'You don't know him. He'd be terrified.'

'And you're not?' asked Iggy.

Umily didn't answer. She went back to destroying the grass.

'You seen it, didn't you?' she said. 'When you and your dad went hunting.'

Iggy looked uncomfortable. He hadn't told anyone about the night he and Hubba had been to the forest. It was probably better to keep it a secret.

'Not exactly,' he said. 'We only saw its tracks.'

'What were they like?'

'Big,' said Iggy.

'Oh,' said Umily quietly.

'I don't think it swallows you straight away,' said Iggy. 'First it sort of slobbers over you — covers you in a disgusting dribble, all slimy and sticky so you're half blind. That's probably the worst part . . .'

'Thanks, I get the idea.' Umily had turned even paler than before.

Iggy fumbled inside his furs. 'I nearly forgot, I brought you something.'

'Not more dandelions?'

'No, it's my wolf's tooth necklace. Maybe it'll bring you luck.'

Umily looked at the necklace in his hand. 'Thanks, but I've got one. Snark gave me his.'

She touched the necklace round her neck, which Iggy had somehow failed to notice. It had a small bone carved in the shape of the moon, or possibly a fish, it was hard to tell.

'It's um . . . nice,' said Iggy.

'He says I mustn't worry. He'd never let nothing happen to me.'

Iggy's eyes widened. 'Snark said that?'

'Yes. He's the bravest person I know.'

'Mmm,' said Iggy. Snark was certainly the biggest liar he knew.

He got up to go. Umily stood up as well.

'Well,' said Iggy, 'see you then.'

He trudged back up the hill, wishing a boulder would drop on his head from the sky.

'*See you then.*' What kind of idiot said that to someone who was about to die?

*

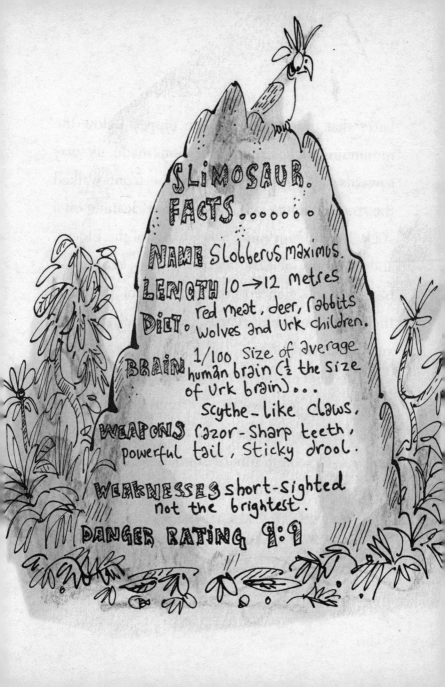

SLIMOSAUR. FACTS........

NAME Slobberus maximus.

LENGTH 10→12 metres

DIET red meat, deer, rabbits wolves and Urk children.

BRAIN 1/100 size of average human brain (½ the size of Urk brain)...

WEAPONS Scythe-like claws. razor-sharp teeth, powerful tail, sticky drool.

WEAKNESSES short-sighted not the brightest.

DANGER RATING 9:9

Later that evening, as the sun dipped below the mountains, a solemn procession made its way towards the Forest of Urk. At the front walked the stooped figure of Gaga the Wise, leaning on a stick. Behind him came Borg, Chief of the Elders, and a group of Urk warriors who kept close together and glanced constantly about them. At the back, flanked by guards, came Umily, looking very small and alone.

From high on the hill, Iggy and Hubba watched the procession cross the river and approach the trees. Iggy was busy knotting together long bits of sinew – the tough bits of animals that are useful for making weapons or knotting together.

'What you call it again?' asked Hubba.

'A net,' said Iggy.

'Oh. Funny name. What's it for then?'

'You throw it,' said Iggy.

'Like a spear, you mean? Where's the pointy bit?'

'This is different. The animal gets caught in the net and it struggles but it can't escape.'

Hubba laughed. 'Course it can! You left whoppin' big big holes! It'll wriggle out.'

'No, it won't!' said Iggy.

'A snake would. Or a worm.'

'It won't wriggle out,' said Iggy irritably. 'Once it's caught, it can't get away.'

'Show us then,' demanded Hubba.

'I told you, it's not finished yet.'

'But just show us how it works.'

Iggy sighed. He bunched up the net and threw it high, so it landed neatly over Hubba's head. Hubba shook himself like a dog and the net fell in a heap on the grass. Iggy picked it up.

'Like I said, it's not finished yet.'

Meanwhile, deep in the forest, the procession had come to a halt. The light was fading and it had begun to rain. The Urks were unwilling to go any further. Since entering the woods they had become more and more nervous, and several were convinced that the trees were following them. They stood watching as Gaga the Wise led Umily to an old, twisted oak tree and tied her to the trunk.

'Any last requests, my child?' he asked gravely.

'Can us come back when it's not raining?' asked Umily.

'I'm afraid not.'

Gaga took a few steps back, spread out his arms and addressed the sky in a loud, ringing voice.

'Great Spirits of the Ancestors, we offer you this Daughter of Urk . . .'

Borg tapped him on the shoulder.

'Do the short version. We're in a hurry.'

Gaga hesitated for a moment. The others were already edging away, anxious to be gone.

'Great Spirits,' he said. 'She's all yours.' He hurried after them. Umily was left alone with only the wind and the rain for company.

Minutes slipped past and became hours. Soon she lost track of how long she'd been there. The leather cords bit into her arms and chafed whenever she struggled. As darkness came she began to hear noises. Rustling, scuffling, snuffling noises. A twig snapped. The trees moaned in the wind. Umily closed her eyes and tried to pretend she was safe at home in her cave. Her eyes blinked open. Something was coming. In the moonlight she thought she glimpsed a shadow flitting silently between the trees. She struggled wildly, desperate to break free. She wanted to cry out for help, but her mouth was dry as a bone. Somewhere in the darkness *IT* was watching her, waiting to pounce.

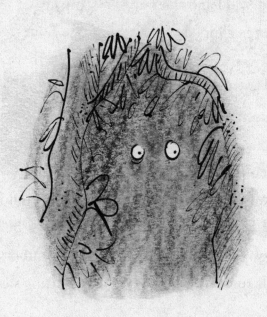

Chapter 8
Saving Umily

'YAAAARGHHHHHH!'

Umily screamed as the thing leapt out from behind a tree.

'Iggy, you bonehead!' she groaned. 'You scared me half to death!'

Iggy blinked. To be honest he'd expected more of a welcome. After all, he was risking his life — and it was raining.

'What're you doing here?' asked Umily.

'I came to save you.'

'*You?*'

'Yes. Well, me and Hubba. He's back there.'

'Hello, Umily!' Hubba's head popped up from the bushes and he waved cheerily.

Umily wondered if this was a dream.

'Anyway, you're all right,' said Iggy.

'All right? I'm wet through and tied to a tree!'

'Yes, I know, but you're alive. And look, I brought something.'

Iggy showed her a strange knotted thing that he

had slung over his shoulder. It looked like a moth-
eaten blanket.

'It's a net,' he said. 'For catching slimosaurs.
It's stronger than it looks. You hold it like this . . .'

'IGGY!' cried Umily. 'We don't have time!'

'Oh yes, sorry. I'd better cut you loose.' He
slipped a hand inside his furs and felt around.
'Oh.'

'Now what?' said Umily.

'I forgot to bring an axe.'

Umily hung her head in despair. This was probably the worst rescue of all time.

'Don't worry,' said Iggy. 'I can probably bite
through it.'

He tested the leather cords with his teeth, but

they were much too thick.

'Stay there,' he said. 'I'll be right back.'

He hadn't got more than a few steps when he froze in his tracks. It was the same noise they'd heard the night they were picking yumberries. A low, blood-curdling roar that carried on the wind and filled the forest with squawks and shrieks.

'GROOARGHHHHHHHH!'
THUD . . . THUD . . . THUD!

The slimosaur was on the move, making the ground shake.

'Iggy!' cried Umily. 'Where are you?'

No answer came back. Iggy had vanished into the darkness, abandoning her.

THUD . . . THUD . . . THUD!

It was coming closer. Where was Snark? Snark the Fearless, who would protect her?

Close by, Hubba and Iggy were watching from their hiding place in the middle of a holly bush.

'Ow! It prickles!' grumbled Hubba.

'Then keep still!'

'I *am* keeping still! Do you see anything?'

'No,' hissed Iggy. 'It's too dark.'

They listened. The forest had gone as silent as a graveyard. All they could hear was Umily's snuffly breathing. In the darkness, Iggy could hardly see her under the tree. They had brought a torch, but the rain had practically put out the flame.

THUD . . . THUD . . . THUD!

The monster was coming. Iggy wondered if it could smell them on the breeze. It would be easy enough to smell Hubba.

'Remember,' hissed Iggy. 'Wait till it's caught in the net.'

'Then we run?' asked Hubba.

'No. Then we kill it.'

'Right. What if the net don't hold it?'

'It will,' said Iggy.

'But what if it don't?'

'*Then* we run.'

Iggy peered into the darkness, one hand grasping the net and the other gripping his spear. He wondered if hunting was always like this – a mixture of terror, excitement and wishing it would stop raining. Suddenly the forest shook again. A monstrous head loomed into view, outlined against the moon. The next thing Iggy heard was Umily's scream and he burst from the bushes with Hubba at his heels.

What happened next was all panic and confusion as they lost sight of each other in the dark. Iggy came upon the slimosaur from behind and leapt back as the long green tail almost knocked him off his feet.

'IGGY!'

He heard Umily scream again, followed by another sound like a wave of custard splatting against a wall. Iggy rushed towards the noise and stumbled against something on the ground. He threw the net.

'Hubba! I've got it!'

The beast kicked and struggled to escape. Iggy raised his spear and jabbed down hard.

'OWW!' yelped the beast. 'Get off, you noggerhead!'

It wasn't the slimosaur. It was Hubba who was blundering around in the net.

'Hubba! Where is it?' cried Iggy.

'Don't ask me! I fell over.'

Hubba managed to untangle himself from the net and rubbed his bottom where the spear had prodded him. They both looked around, suddenly aware that the roaring in their ears had stopped. A distant booming told them that the slimosaur was lumbering off through the forest. Leaves and broken branches littered the ground.

'Umily!' said Iggy, realising they'd forgotten all about her. He hurried to the twisted oak, suddenly afraid what he might find. Umily had gone. All that was left was a patch of sticky gloop dripping

down the tree trunk and forming a thick green puddle in the mud. Iggy covered his face with his hands and turned away.

'Don't look,' he said. 'We're too late.'

Chapter 9

Lair of the Slimosaur

Hubba crouched down and dabbed a finger in the slime.

'Hmmm,' he said.

Iggy looked at him. 'What do you mean, "Hmmm"?'

'Well, look – where's her bones?' asked Hubba. 'If she'd been eaten, there'd be bones and innards.'

Iggy cast around under the tree. Hubba was

right. The day they had followed the slimosaur's trail it had led them to a fly-ridden pile of bones. But there was no trace of Umily at all. It was as if she'd vanished in a puff of smoke – or in this case a puddle of slime.

'Then maybe she got away,' suggested Iggy.

Hubba looked doubtful. 'Maybe. Or it carried her off.'

'Why would it do that?'

Hubba shrugged. 'Don't ask me. To get out of the rain?' Figuring things out was supposed to be Iggy's job.

They searched the muddy ground for tracks. There was no sign of Umily's footprints, but it wasn't hard to tell which direction the slimosaur had taken — it looked as if a giant boulderball had cut a path through the trees.

For the next hour they followed the trail by the moonlight and the faint glow of Iggy's torch. Further on, in the muddy shallows of a stream, Iggy found two large footprints. Something small and white under the water caught his eye. He fished it out. It was Umily's bone necklace, the one that Snark had given her. They had come this way. If Umily was alive, maybe she'd dropped it deliberately, hoping they would follow the trail.

Finally the forest began to thin out and it was easier to see their way. They emerged into a barren rocky valley. Steep hills rose up either side of a dry riverbed strewn with boulders shaped like giant eggs. Iggy trod on something sharp, which made a loud crunch. He stooped to pick up an animal skull, now badly dented and missing a few teeth.

'Nice,' said Hubba.

Further on they came across more piles of bones: claws, beaks and grinning skulls. Iggy looked round uneasily.

'Are you thinking what I'm thinking?'

Hubba frowned. 'Dunno. I weren't thinking.'

'This is its lair, Hubba. I think we've found it.'

They went on more carefully, clambering over

rocks and taking care not to step on any bones. Turning a corner, Iggy stopped dead. Slowly he raised a finger and pointed to a humpbacked hill just ahead. Curiously the hill was covered in scales and rose and fell in time with raspy breathing. The slimosaur was asleep.

They backed up and circled the beast, giving it a wide berth. When they were level with the head, they hid behind some rocks to watch it from a safe distance. The slimosaur was flopped on its belly. A trail of slime drooled from one side of its mouth. Iggy noticed blood on its teeth and a cold shudder went through him. But Umily wasn't dead. The creature had her gripped in one of its claws. She seemed unharmed, though she was coated in thick green gunk. Hubba jumped to his feet.

'Wait!' said Iggy, pulling him down. 'If it wakes up now, we're all dead. We've got to get close without disturbing it.'

'Then what?' said Hubba.

'Then we grab Umily and get out of here.'

They crept closer. Umily gave no sign she'd seen them, although it was probably difficult to wave when you were in the grip of a giant claw. Iggy crept from one boulder to the next till they were almost at the head. The slimosaur's eyes remained closed, its breath turning the air sour. Iggy crept over to Umily and softly whispered her name. Her eyes blinked open in amazement. Iggy put a finger to his lips. Kneeling down, he tried to

pull her out by the arms, but the claw only tight-
ened its grip. The slimosaur grunted in its sleep
and let out a horrible belch.

'BUUUUUUURRROOOP!'

'Iggy! Hurry up!' hissed Hubba.

'I'm trying!'

Iggy cast around for a solution. Piles of bones
lay everywhere and beside one was a heap of
brown feathers. It gave him an idea. He chose the
largest feather he could find and took it to Umily.
She stared at him blankly.

'Tickle it,' he whispered.

'What?'

'Just try it! Go on, tickle its claw.'

Umily wriggled her arm until she managed to

get in the right position. Using the tip of the feather, she tickled the creature's horny palm. The slimosaur twitched and a gurgling noise bubbled up from its belly. It was laughing. But this wasn't much help since the claw was squeezing Umily tighter. Fighting for breath, she tried again. This time the claw relaxed a fraction, just enough for Iggy to drag her free.

Umily got unsteadily to her feet and took a few deep breaths.

'Can you walk?' Iggy whispered.

She nodded.

They set off, scrabbling over the rocks in the direction they'd come from. Iggy knew if they could just reach the top of the hill they'd be out of

sight. They might have made it too, if Hubba had
looked where he was walking.

'EUGHHH!' he yelled.

Iggy wheeled around. Hubba was staring down
at his foot, which was caked in something brown.
He had stepped in a giant pile of slimosaur droppings.

'Ugh! It stinks!' he moaned, hopping around
on one foot.

Iggy ran back. 'Never mind that. Let's get out
of here.'

'Iggy . . . !'

But Umily's cry of warning
was drowned out . . .

The slimosaur had woken up. It rose to its full towering height, threw back its head and bellowed at the sky again.

'GROOOARRGH!'

Iggy gulped. Hubba took a step back and heard a squelch.

'RUUUUUUUN!'

Chapter 10
A Long Way Down

They ran. Iggy didn't have to look back to know the slimosaur was giving chase. The ground shook and the rocks bounced around like jumping beans. Umily was up ahead and running for her life. Though they had a good head start, the slimosaur was already gaining. Every giant step it took ate up the ground between them. Their only chance was to reach the top of the hill and find somewhere to hide. The steep slope made running hard work, but Iggy drew level with Umily.

'Where's Hubba?' she panted.

He glanced back. Hubba was holding his side and struggling to keep up. Behind him, the slimosaur had reached the bottom of the hill and was beginning to climb. Iggy dashed back and grabbed Hubba by the hand.

'Come on! Hurry!'

'I can't!'

The slimosaur's foot came down on a young tree, flattening it like a mushroom. It roared with fury. Hubba heard it and shook Iggy off, suddenly finding a new burst of energy. Seconds later the two of them raced over the hill to where Umily stood waiting for them. She blocked their path, spreading her arms wide.

'STOP!' she yelled.

Iggy skidded to halt and grabbed Hubba just in the nick of time. They were standing on a flat shelf of rock just a few steps short of the sheer edge of a cliff. When Iggy inched forward to look, the drop made his head swim. They were trapped.

'What now?' moaned Hubba, gasping for breath.

'We fight,' said Umily bravely. 'At least you got your spears.'

Iggy and Hubba looked at each other. In the panic of the escape, they must have dropped their spears when they fled up the hill. All they had was Iggy's net, which now had even more holes than before.

THUD . . . THUD . . . THUD!

Iggy peered over the cliff. If he'd had wings, he could have launched himself off the edge and swooped safely to earth. But he didn't have wings, only a net that was no use at all. Unless . . .

He thought quickly. It was insane, but it was their only chance. He turned to the others.

'We have to jump.'

'What?' said Hubba. 'From here?'

'Yes.'

'You're crazy. We'll be killed!'

'We'll be killed if we stay here,' said Iggy. He began breaking the knots of the net, unpicking it hurriedly. THUD! The ground shook again.

'Hubba, take off your skins,' he ordered.

Hubba blinked at him. 'Eh?'

'Your skins, quickly, I need them!'

'I'm wearing 'em!' protested Hubba. 'There's girls watching!'

Umily rolled her eyes. 'Just do what he says!'

The slimosaur's head loomed into view over the hill. Next came its short stubby arms and its not so stubby body. It lumbered towards them, snarling and drooling. Iggy and Hubba darted behind a boulder and hurriedly stripped off the skins they were wearing. Umily stood her ground and picked up a rock. With all her strength, she hurled it at the beast's head, striking it a lucky blow on the snout. The slimosaur bellowed with rage.

'ROOOOARRRRRGHHHH!'

'Uh-oh,' muttered Umily. She scoured the ground for more ammunition, but there were no more rocks. She backed towards the cliff edge.

'Iggy!' she wailed. 'Hurry up!'

The slimosaur scented a three-course dinner. Umily could see rows of jagged teeth in its mouth. Drool dripped from its jaws and she knew a second wave of slime was on the way.

'Don't look!' cried Iggy, suddenly appearing with Hubba. Umily just had time to register that he was naked apart from something tied round his chest and dragging behind him like a cloak. Iggy pressed a piece of the net into her hand. 'Tie this round yourself. And whatever you do, hold on!'

The slimosaur advanced, crouching with its claws poised to strike. Iggy took another step back, till he was teetering on the edge of the cliff. Hubba had his eyes shut, partly from terror and partly because he was naked and holding hands with a girl.

Iggy looked up at the slimosaur and goaded him. 'Come on, then, Slobberchops! Do it!'

As the slimosaur leapt at them, Iggy, Hubba and Umily dropped over the edge into pitch black darkness.

ARGHHHHHHHH! . . .

Iggy felt the air rush past and his head spun. The thought came to him that tomorrow, or the day after, his parents would find his naked body. At least he didn't have to worry that Umily would see it, because she would be dead too.

. . . ARGHHHHHHHHHHHHH!

Something huge and green hurtled past them in a hail of stones and a second later there was a deafening crunch. Almost at the same instant, Iggy felt a sharp tug on his shoulders. Above him he heard a loud FLUMP! as the skins opened out exactly like a parachute. Dangling below him were Umily and Hubba, hanging on to the net and looking up in bug-eyed astonishment.

A moment later Hubba floated gracefully to earth like a leaf – just before Umily and Iggy landed on top of him in an untidy heap.

'Arghhh! Oww! Get off!' There was a messy struggle as they untangled themselves and tunnelled their way out from under the skins.

Iggy stood up. The first thing he noticed was the slimosaur. Having the body of a giant but the brain of a pea, it had charged straight over the cliff, landing with such a thud that people in the Valley of Urk thought the Spirits of the Ancestors

had fallen out of
bed. The lifeless
beast was now lying
face down in a hole
the size of a swim-
ming pool.

Hubba grabbed Iggy
by the shoulders. 'You
did it, Iggy! We flied!'

'I never thought it
would work!' grinned Iggy.
'It must be like dandelions . . .'

'Who cares?' yelled Hubba,
who wasn't in the mood for a science
lesson. 'We're alive! We killed the slimosaur!

Wait till they hear this!'

'Um, didn't you forget something?'

It was Umily who spoke. She had one hand over her eyes. Iggy and Hubba looked at her, puzzled, then looked down at their feet as it dawned on them. They weren't wearing *anything at all*.

'ARGHHHHHHH!'

Chapter 11
Heads, You Lose

C hief Hammerhead was roused from a deep sleep by someone shaking him by the shoulder.

'W-what?' he mumbled.

'Hammy, wake up, you big lump!' said a voice.

A hand grabbed his leg, trying to drag him out from under his furs. He put up strong resistance.

'Leave me 'lone!'

'Get up, Hammy! They're back!' said Iggy's dad. 'And they got Umily!'

Hammerhead buried his head under his furs. 'Umily's dead!' he moaned. 'Dead! Dead! And all my fault!'

'She's not dead, you dunghill!' cried Iggy's dad. 'I just seen her.'

'Umily?'

'That's what I'm telling you! She's outside. Come and see for yourself!'

Hammerhead wrapped his furs around him, and emerged from his cave, blinking in the early-morning light. He pushed his way through the large crowd that had gathered on the hillside. Coming up the slope, he could see Iggy and Hubba, dragging something heavy behind them. Beside them walked a girl with green hair sticking up like a spiky hedgehog. Hammerhead would have known his daughter anywhere. He rushed down to meet her.

There were tears and hugs and more tears – mostly from the Chief. The Urks crowded round to listen as Iggy recounted their adventures – how they had tracked the slimosaur to its lair and rescued Umily (missing out the part about jumping off a cliff stark naked).

'But what about the slimosaur?' asked Hammerhead, when Iggy paused for breath.

'Oh, I nearly forgot,' said Iggy. 'Hubba, give me a hand.'

They dragged the net over and tipped it up. Out rolled the scaly head of the slimosaur and

landed at the Chief's feet.

'Blood and thunder!' cried Hammerhead. 'You killed it?'

'Well, not by myself,' said Iggy. 'We did it together.'

'But Iggy saved our lives,' said Umily.

'You fought it off,' said Iggy. 'You were braver than me.'

'No, I weren't.'

'Yes, you were.'

'Oh, for Urk's sake!' groaned Hubba. If this

carried on, they'd soon be holding hands.

That evening the Urks held the greatest feast in living memory, a feast that went on long into the night with drumming, dancing and large helpings of roast slimosaur for everyone. But before the feasting began, there was another event. Iggy's boulderball team, the Elks, challenged the Rhinos to a rematch.

The tribe gathered on the hill eager to see if the tribal champions could be beaten. Once again Iggy went forward for the toss of the lizard and watched it spin in the air. This time, however, it didn't hit the mud because he reached out a hand

and caught it.

'Call,' he said. 'Heads or tails?'

'That's not fair!' grumbled Snark. 'I can't see it!'

'Then you won't be able to cheat. Heads or tails?' repeated Iggy.

Snark looked at his dad sulkily. 'Heads,' he said. 'No, tails! Heads! Tails . . . HEADS!'

'Sure now?' said Iggy. 'Don't want to change your mind?'

Snark shook his head. He knew when someone was trying to trick him. Iggy removed his top hand. The lizard lay struggling on its back.

'Sorry, it's tails.' Iggy grinned. 'We get the slope.'

*

The two teams took up their positions at opposite ends of the hill. Iggy glanced at his team: Hubba beside him, Fleabit looking nervous, and Umily, their newest recruit, with her hair knotted in a bone.

'Remember what we said?' asked Iggy.

They all nodded.

BAWOOOM!

The horn sounded and Snark's team set off up the slope like a herd of stampeding buffalo. The Elks didn't move. Iggy and his team-mates stood behind their boneposts, deaf to the shouts urging them forward.

Sensing their advantage, the Rhinos reached the boulder, a giant hulka. They strained and groaned, sweated and heaved. Finally the boulder shifted and rolled over. They began inching it slowly up the hill, Snark driving his team on with threats and curses. Step by slow step they covered the slope, getting nearer to their opponents' goal. Still Iggy didn't speak or move. His team stood like statues.

At last the Rhinos reached the top of the hill, only one last push from the posts. They stopped to rest a moment, steaming and panting like carthorses.

'PUSH!' yelled Snark. 'One more push!'

They sweated and grunted, but the boulder refused to budge. It was stuck.

Hubba looked at Iggy. 'Now?'

'Now,' said Iggy.

They launched themselves at the boulder, taking their opponents by surprise. It took just one big push before the rock lurched and began to roll back down the hill.

'HOLD IT!' screamed Snark. But his teammates had scattered in panic. Snark pelted down the hill, with the speeding boulder giving chase.

'DAD!' he squawked. 'HEEEELP!'

Next moment the boulder caught up with him, carrying him down the slope like a spider stuck to a giant snowball. Over and over, faster and faster, it rolled, crashing between the boneposts and heading on towards the river.

'BOULDER!' roared the crowd over the noise of the mighty splash.

Iggy dusted off his hands. It had been a long time coming, but it was definitely worth the wait.

And **Iggy the Urk's** caveboy capers will continue in April 2011!

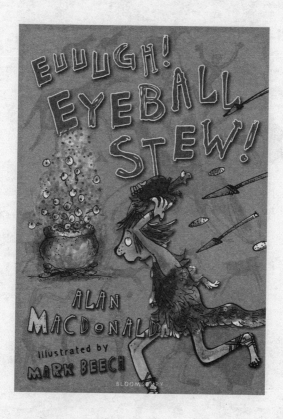

By the same author

TROMP YOUR WAY THROUGH THE DISGRACEFULLY DISGUSTING

TROLL TROUBLE

BOOKS

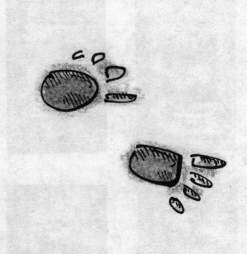

Also by Alan MacDonald

HISTORY of WARTS

Custardly Wart
Pirate (Third Class)
ALAN MacDONALD

Ditherus Wart
(Accidental) Gladiator
ALAN MacDONALD

Honesty Wart
Witch Hunter!
ALAN MacDONALD

Sir Bigwart
Knight of the Wonky Table
ALAN MacDONALD

To order direct from Bloomsbury Publishing visit www.bloomsbury.com/alanmacdonald
or call 020 7440 2475

www.bloomsbury.com